Puppy Takes a Bath

by Christine Ricci
illustrated by Tom Mangano

Ready-to-Read

SCHOLASTIC INC.
New York Toronto London Auckland Sydney
Mexico City New Delhi Hong Kong Buenos Aires

Based on the TV series *Dora the Explorer*® as seen on Nick Jr.®

No part of this publication may be reproduced, stored in a retrieval system, or
transmitted in any form or by any means, electronic, mechanical, photocopying,
recording, or otherwise, without written permission of the publisher. For
information regarding permission, write to Simon Spotlight, Simon & Schuster
Children's Publishing Division, 1230 Avenue of the Americas, New York, NY 10020.

ISBN 0-439-87031-3

Copyright © 2006 by Viacom International Inc. NICK JR., *Dora the Explorer*,
and all related titles, logos, and characters are registered trademarks
of Viacom International Inc. All rights reserved. Published by Scholastic Inc.,
557 Broadway, New York, NY 10012, by arrangement with Simon Spotlight,
Simon & Schuster Children's Publishing Division. SCHOLASTIC and associated
logos are trademarks and/or registered trademarks of Scholastic Inc.

12 11 10 9 8 7 6 5 4 3 2 1   6 7 8 9 10 11/0

Printed in the U.S.A.

First Scholastic printing, September 2006

READY-TO-READ is a registered trademark of Simon & Schuster, Inc.

Hi! I am Dora.

This is my puppy.

My puppy loves
to roll in the dirt.

My puppy needs a bath!

Here is a tub of water.

Backpack has the soap
and the towel.

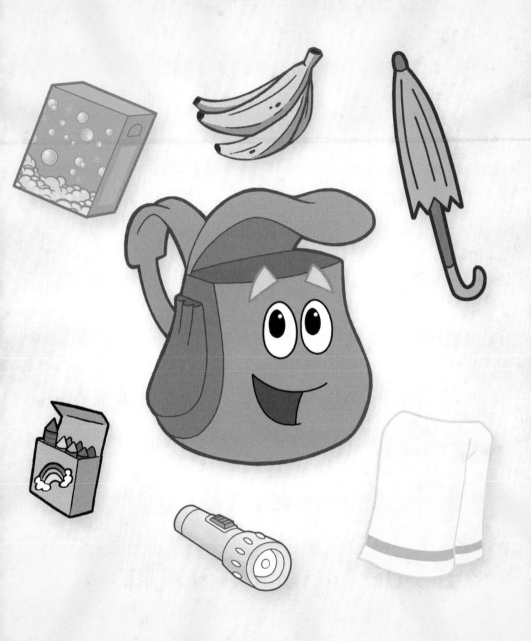

Help me find them!

The bath is ready.

But where is my puppy?

Is my puppy

hiding in the bushes?

No! My puppy is not
in the bushes.

Is my puppy hiding
in the flowers?

No! My puppy is not
in the flowers.

Is my puppy hiding
in the doghouse?

No! My puppy is not
in the doghouse.

I have an idea!

Here is a bone.

Here is my puppy!

My puppy sees the bone.

My puppy likes his bath.

My puppy is all clean!